A catalogue record for this book is available from
the British Library.

First edition

Published by Ladybird Books Ltd Loughborough Leicestershire UK
Ladybird Books Inc Auburn Maine 04210 USA
Printed in England (3)

LADYBIRD FIRST READERS

wheels

by JACQUELINE HARDING
illustrated by GAYNOR CHAPMAN

Ladybird Books

In the morning the dustcart came to take the rubbish.

dustcart

The lady missed
the bus.
What will she do?

bus

This truck had to stop at the side of the road!

truck

The big car towing
the caravan drove
round the truck.

caravan   car

A horse trotted down
the road.
The motorbike went
past carefully.

motorbike

The tractor went slowly
along the road.

tractor

That car was going too fast!

car

Beep! Beep!
The taxi was in a
hurry but there was
too much traffic.

taxi

A pickup truck broke down in the middle of the road.

pickup truck

A man helped to push the truck to the side of the road so that the traffic could get through.

traffic

A man in a
breakdown truck
came to look.

breakdown truck

So much traffic moving slowly ...except

the boy on his bike!